# PETITE'S WINTER WONDERLAND

By Amy Sky Koster

Illustrated by the Disney Storybook Art Team

A Random House PICTUREBACK® Book

Random House 🏠 New York

randomhousekids.com    ISBN 978-0-7364-3355-6

MANUFACTURED IN CHINA

10 9 8 7 6 5 4 3 2 1

Glitter effect and production: Red Bird Publishing Ltd., U.K.

Petite the pony loved winter! She loved the pure white snow, the crisp air, and racing through the frosty forest.

But winter was cold.

One day, when Petite was out in the woods, she found herself wishing she had a warm stable to go home to. There were no barns in sight, so she headed toward a clearing in the hope that the sun would warm her instead.

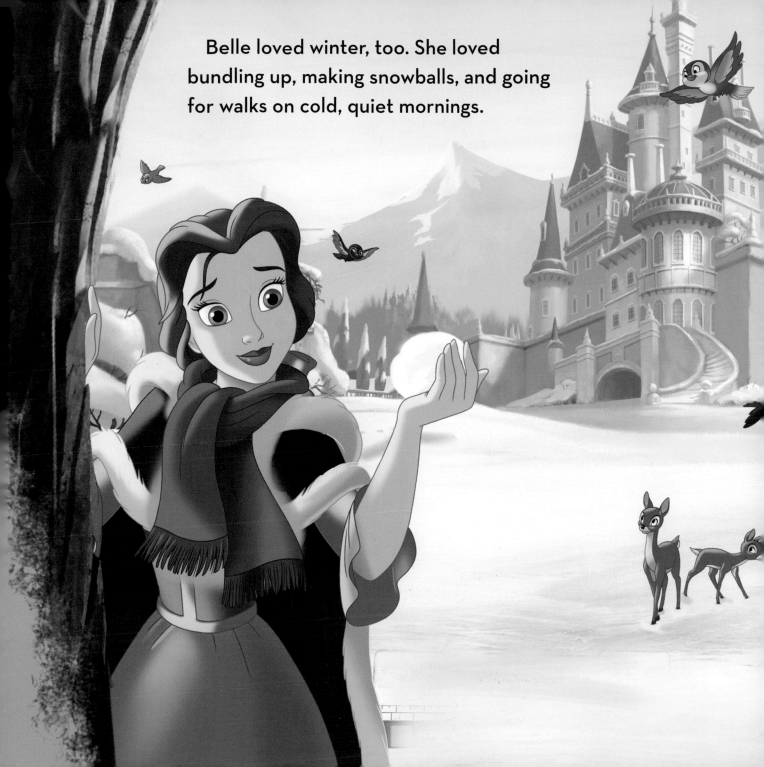

Belle loved winter, too. She loved bundling up, making snowballs, and going for walks on cold, quiet mornings.

Most of all, Belle loved to ice-skate!
One day, she was performing twirls and figure
eights for an audience of forest animals.

After a while, Belle noticed someone else watching her skate—a sweet little pony on the other side of the lake!

Petite grew nervous when she saw the princess skating
toward her. The little pony was wary of strangers.

Belle approached Petite slowly and pulled
a few sugar cubes from her pocket. The little
pony loved sugary treats!

Soon Petite was munching on the sugar cubes while Belle stroked the pony's mane.

"*Brr!* It's cold!" said Belle as she wrapped a scarf around Petite's neck. "Let's go home."

Home! Petite was so excited!

Belle skated back across the ice. Petite ran beside her along the frozen lake.

Belle performed a few more twirls and figure eights.
She even did a little jump. Next to her, Petite leaped, too!

Petite met Belle on the other side of the lake, and together the new friends walked through the woods toward the castle. Along the way, they kicked up soft snow and caught snowflakes on their tongues.

When they arrived at the royal stable, Belle brushed
the snowflakes from Petite's mane and covered her with
a cozy blanket.

"Welcome home," Belle whispered as Petite nuzzled her.
Now Belle and Petite loved winter even more!